"You cannot find peace by avoiding life."

— *Virginia Woolf*

Portraits Of Girls I Never Met

Rebecca Rijsdijk

To Annelies

CONTENTS

Acknowledgments

About the Author

ACKNOWLEDGMENTS

I just wanted to say thank you, to my mother, for always reading everything that I write. To Gerard and Vicky for believing in me in the early years, when I made messes that were too big for me to clean up and I ended up turning us all into characters and stories in order to deal with things. Thanks Roberto, for believing in me before I believed in myself. Thank you Sofia and George for your feedback in the early stages of going public. Thank you Fran, for pushing me when I felt like giving up. Thank you Rhys for proofreading my earlier drafts. I love you all. This one is for you.

Peanut Butter Sandwiches

The girl tilted her head a little
so that she could see
what he was up to.
She had to squint her eyes
to keep the sun out.

He smiled at her,
even though she could not find
a reason for him to do so.

She was happy when he smiled.

"There is peanut butter on your
jumper," he said.

She looked at the direction
his finger was pointing at.

There was a smudge right on the spot
where a breast used to be.

"Yes," she replied,
and that was that
the smudge turned
into a stain.

Stockholm Syndrome

She had been laying there for a while,
with her arms wide spread
in the middle of the room.
The tones her radio produced
no longer satisfying her.

She thought about leaving.
She thought about having kids.
She thought about taking a trip
to Canada, or Mexico,
anywhere but here.

Her eyes were closed
but she could picture the room clearly;
the empty spots on the chimney
and the dust on the floor.

Since he had left she was not able
to organise her thoughts any more.
They were just floating there,
inside of her, leaving her head,
spreading through her limbs.

So much anger.

She thought about smashing
his portrait into a wall,
but she did not feel like
picking up the pieces afterwards.

And the Sun was shining underneath the Bed Sheets

"I don't love you anymore."
She tried reading his eyes
but he had lowered his head
and was staring at the warm sheets
they had just made love under.

The room went silent for a while,
leaving them nothing but drops of
sweat on naked skin and half smoked
cigarettes in an overflowing ashtray.

He expected her to yell at him, kick
him out of the bed like she had done so
many times before,
but she just sat there
and bit her lip.

The Cliffs of Dover and how Mary wouldn't leave her House when it came tumbling down

She was nervous,
I could tell by the way her head moved,
her eyes frantically avoiding mine,
the speed with which she talked.

I pictured her children
and how they had abandoned her
after she turned a certain age.

Their portraits on her wall
like the trophy heads of animals.

It was wonderful once,
but today the cliffs
were slowly disappearing
into the sea,
as Mary wouldn't leave her house
when it came tumbling down.

My Old Man

He looked at his hands,
more wrinkles appeared every day.
He had given up
looking at his face
a while ago,
as he made a habit of it
to avoid mirrors and windows.

People only changed on the outside.
As had the village he grew up in.

My father was standing in the spot
where his father had taught him
how to ride a bike.

The view had changed a bit.

It hardly seems fair that you get to go back to your miserably comfortable life, while I wake up with a hangover every day.

I wait for you, another summer.
"It is not just me," you say,
"it is your job too."

I look at the garden
from behind the glass.
Summer passes by swiftly
when you are a part of it.

"My job?" I ask,
watching a blue tit land
on the patch of grass where they
scattered M's ashes.
The grass was getting long.

"You disappear,
sometimes for weeks on end."

My lips don't move
until after they start bleeding.

"So do you," I sigh,
"even when we are in the same room."

Empty Rooms

She looked at the hotel,
which no longer was a hotel
but a couple of empty rooms,
kept together by a hole in the roof
as she carried around a key chain
which contained the keys
to buildings which
no longer existed.

Rebecca Rijsdijk

The Girl with
the pretty Face

It was dark in the room;
she liked it like that nowadays.
She had passed eighty
and her face started to show
signs of death
as she clung on to life;
in a mausoleum of photographs.
Her gran-daughter brushed her hair
as her tea got cold.
"I cannot get used
to the amount of dead people
on a Monday morning,"
she sighed
as the stretcher rolled
past the window
and into the hearse.

Curly-haired Boy

"Every now and then
it feels like I'm not here,
or not really, anyway,"
she said while she cut his hair.

The curls she cut off were as wild on
the floor as they had been on his head.

"Sometimes, when you're like that,"
he replied, "you can look at me
without seeing me."

The white curtains they had bought at
the local market last Monday
came flying in.

"It is almost like you are someone else."

She handed him the scissors
and closed the window.

"That is exactly what it feels like."

Summertime

Sounds of the summer;
the closing of doors
that desperately want to be open;
screaming children on the top floor;
a woman yelling at her dog because it
was chasing a pigeon.

The sun fooled the daffodils this year
and spring arrived earlier than usual.

More sounds of the summer.

Just as she notices how thirsty she is,
he brings her a glass of lemonade.
She watches him leave
as she brings the glass to her mouth.

"You're beautiful," she says,
with one eye pinched
and her head tilted in such a way
that she could just make out his shape
in the darkened room.

Cunt

I nicked her last cigarette
because I hoped
it would unsettle
the fuck out of her
when she woke up.

Of Dying Plants and Cigarettes

She licked her lips as she stared into the distance. The wind blew the rain against the window with such force that it startled her from time to time. The boy opposite of her killed his smoke in the flowerpot next to the couch. "Do you know that feeling," she paused, letting her hand slide down the arm of her chair, "that feeling that you are better off alone when you spend too much time among other people?" She glanced briefly into nothingness before turning her gaze in his direction. He was busy pulling the leaves of a plant that was about to die. "All the time," he said and stuck his chewing gum against the side of his glass, "all the fucking time."

Reoccurring dream

She had a reoccurring dream of herself
on bare feet, running through the hills
with her arms wide open.
The sunbeams that made it through the
thick foliage above her head, warmed
her face. This had to be the place.

Virginia

I saw you cross my street
the other day.
You were with this beautiful boy
and you were smiling.
Your cheeks were flushed
and the fabric of your dress
was covered with flowers.

I wondered what it would be like
to be you for a day.

The boy took your hand
just as you looked back at me,
your long hair all tangled and
beautiful; touched by the sun
that was about to go down,
golden light, the best light of the day.

You waved at me
while I put the kettle on.

I stepped away
from the kitchen window
and watched you disappear
into the distance.

You looked like a Virginia to me.

Dear Dead Boy

I could see you standing there with one
hand in your pocket and your messy
hair. I didn't dare turn my head entirely
in your direction because deep down I
knew, you were actually dead.

Shoreline

It was dark at sea;
the only lights you could navigate on
were the dim ones on the pier.

Last night's snow
had given the beach
her virginity back.

It was colder
than the weatherman
had predicted; wilder.

It was like the ocean
was attempting
to swallow up the land
and everything on it.

The black water tried its best
to conquer the coastline
and the wind kept changing direction.

Bursts of cold air
swept in their faces
and he did his best
to endure her company.

Thursday Night

"When we stand next to each other,
you can still surprise me
with the things you see,"
she said when she saw
that she had run out of smokes.
He was sitting on her right side
and was playing with his telephone.
In his free hand he held hers.
He loved her
even when she was drunk.

Hopes and Dreams

"I dreamed about you last night."
The image is blurry; back light
obstructing a clear view; a dark hallway
with daylight pouring in through the
front door as the only source of light.
"I dreamed that you were happy."
Music softly plays in the background.
The image becomes clearer, an
elderly lady stands in front of a mirror.
She studies her own face. A younger
woman applies lipstick to the older
woman's lips. "You were young and
beautiful, on a beach somewhere with
your legs crossed, leaning back on your
hands in the sand." She brushes away
the remains of a mistake just above the
upper lip. "You had that look on your
face, taunting, the one you always used
to get your way, the one that turned
your ex husbands into idiots."
The younger woman gets the elderly
lady's coat. "I wish I had known you
back then, full of hopes and dreams.
I wish I had known you back then
before your heart turned ugly and cold.

The Things I do
when You are not Home

Wear your t-shirts,
Drink coffee from your favourite mug,
Sleep on your side of the bed,
Smell your pillow,
Masturbate in the shower.

Aneurysm

It was just another sunny afternoon,
like the seven afternoons that had
come before it. I remember new life in
the meadows and pollen in the air.
It was early May and I did not need a
coat. I had just told you I would
probably be late again as little drops
of sweat started to form on my brow.
"You're a shit journalist," you replied.
Your tone wasn't irritated, but a little
bit amused. "You're probably right."
By the time I neared the end of our
street, the drops of sweat on my
forehead had become rivers. I closed
my eyes, I couldn't help it, they had
never felt heavier. I fell and bled,
but the bleeding only occurred on the
inside of my head. People take you less
serious if they can't see the red
pouring out.

Poem for the Pig upstairs

I hate you.
Please die.

Rebecca Rijsdijk

Kathmandu Valley

The journey had come to a halt at a
place where you could still see the stars
after the sun goes down. He walked
onto the porch and lit a cigarette.
The smoke he exhaled disappeared in
the direction of the great black canvas
above his head. There were no stars
where he was from; there was only
light pollution.

The Heroine / Germaine

He walked out, in the middle of winter;
snow was covering the pavement and
the sun shone brightly. She watched
the steam coming from his lips for a
second before she realized what was
going on. He had no coat on and he
walked in circles. His mind was completely gone by now, the last bit of his
sanity suppressed by the drugs they
were giving him. There was no room
for him at the closed wing yet.
"Let him go," the pigs said. "Let him go,
it is not our responsibility." A woman
with grey streaks in her hair walked
toward the door, not minding what the
pigs were saying. Her steps were
resolute but the yelling of her
colleagues made her eyes twitch.
"This is a human being you're
talking about, not an office appliance."
The woman with the grey streaks in
her hair stood at the door and called
out to him, ignoring the objections of
her work mates. "Mr V. come on in
now, it is too cold outside." He stopped
in his tracks, looked at her without

recognising her, the air around him
filling with his breath. She stuck out
her hand as he slowly started walking
towards her, not saying a word, his face
as pale as the snow surrounding him.
I watched her; the frown on her face;
concern in her eyes. I watched her and
I felt like cheering when he took her
hand and slowly walked inside, but I
didn't. Instead I told her she was one
of the good ones. I whispered it to her
when she passed me later on with her
arms full of plates; the only decent
person in the whole god damned
nursing home.

The City

Shallow breaths at the traffic light.
The muscles in her face looked tight
while the city buzzed around her.
People like ants, pink cheeks, a bright
summer's dress in a sea of black suits
and ties. Her scream doesn't quite
reach the surface. Shallow breaths.
The city chews her up, spits her out.
Shallow breaths, shallow breaths.

Rush Hour

It was rush hour.
The wind wrapped its claws
around my hair
like it always did
when I left Central Station.

Everyone's eyes pointed down,
like looking up would be a crime.

It took me a while
to notice a pair of eyes
that strayed.

They belonged to a woman
in her early forties.
She smiled at me
when she noticed
the way my sweater was buttoned.
I had been in a hurry.

One pair of eyes was enough.

Portrait of A Girl
I Never Met

As she wandered off along the
shoreline, she asked herself why most
people were so afraid of dying, as it
was living that scared her the most.
She thought about her grandmother,
wetting herself in the bed she had been
laid in to die, her hair gone because of
the disease that was spreading through
her limbs. It was getting dark and the
land was disappearing. She did not feel
like going home.

Liar

The shadows of lunacy were roaming
the room as she sat down in a dark
corner, watching the patterns the sun
made on the wall.

"I still love you," he said.
It sounded like a poem.

She liked this version of him, the boy
that went up the mountain and
descended a man. He seemed happy
and sad about it all at the same time.

His fingers appeared on her knee and
she stared at them for a while, trying
not to tremble under the familiarity of
his touch.

His hand burned a hole in her knee
until she finally took it in hers. She told
herself she didn't believe in regret. She
was a terrible liar.

The Boy with the Sun in his Heart

"Do you want to go for a coffee?"
he asked once they had arrived at the
corner of the street. She shook her
head. "I have to go." When she kissed
him on the cheek she couldn't help
but to touch the corners of his mouth.
She had loved many men, but she had
loved him the most.

Royal Blue Mondays

I wanted to tell her it wasn't my fault,
but she looked so angry when she told
me she had enough of my sloppy
handwriting and the mess I made in
my workbooks. I looked at the stains
on the page, royal blue stains, ink
smeared out over the words we were
supposed to copy. She grabbed hold
of my wrist. "Here, do it like this," she
commanded, pressing my arm down
on the table with so much force I
thought her only aim was to break it.
I still, for the life of me, don't
understand why I just didn't tell her my
god damned fountain-pen was leaking.

Doreen

And sometimes
when she does remember,
she calls me her little angel
and she knows where she is
and everything is all right
for a second or a minute
and then we cry;
she for the life that she lost
I for the woman I only know about
through the stories of her children.

The Mole

"Do you have to have something
removed dear?" She smiled at me,
her glasses were stained. I looked at the
people in the waiting room and nodded
to the woman behind the desk. "Yes,
yes I do." It was an odd way to start a
conversation and I could feel my palms
getting sweaty. She looked away from
me, at the computer in front of her.
The glasses were on the tip of her nose
now, like they belonged there for the
task she was about to perform.
We picked a date and I wanted to leave,
started to head out even, away from the
sterile smell and the eyes of the people
in the waiting room. "I need your date
of birth love," she said, her fingers ready
at the keyboard. I turned around and
told her I was born in nineteen eighty
four. Whenever I told people this, they
changed their tones and stopped
treating me like a sixteen year old.
She made the appointment and when I
left the building I thought about all the
things I would have liked to have
removed instead of the little
discoloured mole between my breasts.
I had told the doctor I scar beautifully.

Delia

"We're lost," she said, the wind
sweeping her hat right off her tiny
frozen head. She looks at me with her
glasses on the tip of her nose.
She scares me when she wears them
like that, like an angry school teacher
or a disappointed parent. "You have no
idea where we are, do you?"
The tone in her voice prepares me for
what is coming as I watch her clasp her
walking stick in the angry manner I've
become so used to over the last couple
of weeks. The blood disappears from
her hand when she tightens her grip,
spills right into her mad face. I try to
hold on to the image of her black and
white smile in the album back home, at
the end of this street; the smiles for her
first born, her late husband, the friends
whose names we started erasing from
the telephone book. This angry lady
was a happy lady once, with a life very
similar to my own. She had crossed
borders, she had fallen in love, she had
dreams and aspirations before losing
half of her mind in her early seventies.

They say that in the end only the strong emotions remain; love for the faces she recognized, even if she was no longer able to connect any names to them; angst for the stranger that dragged her across the street in the cold. Except I wasn't a stranger, but just impossible to remember."

Tumbleweed

We parked the car down the road.
The warmth that hit me in the face
when I opened the door was
unexpected. It wrapped itself around
me, jerked me out of the car, dried my
throat. We kept our heads down while
the sand filled the air around us.
Everything was a certain brown grey
here; the sand, the mountains, the
shack that served as a public restroom.
We were on our own out here; not a
soul on the road, no buildings, no cars,
no nothing.
My companions went in the lavatories
first while I walked around the back to
take a look at the mountain in front of
me. When I walked back to the car my
ex lover came strolling my way. He was
picking up pebbles and throwing them
away while he gazed in the distance.
His shirt was blue in a sea of grey.
We watched some tumbleweed rolling
across the plain. "Well how about that,"
he smiled, as he finally looked up.
His eyes were as blue as they ever were,
but there was a sense of

accomplishment in them I had never
noticed before. All of a sudden he was
one of those people who were exactly
where they were supposed to be.
And I was still lost.

Traces

Maria always knocked twice before
turning the key. When she had just
started working as a chambermaid in a
fancy hotel that she could never afford
to stay in herself, she
occasionally forgot to knock.
She walked in on a couple having sex
once and never forgot to knock after
that again. Room 301 was empty today
but the lady who stayed there had
left the music on. It was piano music,
Beethoven's Moonlight Sonata. Maria
only listened to the songs they played
on the popular radio stations. Maria
was a housekeeper because she had
an endless curiosity about the lives of
others. She always felt other
people were doing 'it' right.
They weren't like her, stuck in some
underpaid job, looking after a child
on their own. The lady who stayed in
room 301 was one of her favourites.
She was a regular and always stayed
for at least a month. She reminded
Maria of a film star from the fifties; big
red lips and elegant dresses. They had

talked only once, after Maria had
apologised for disturbing her. They
talked about books while Maria
cleaned the room. There were always
a lot of books around, books and
wine and little scraps of paper. Maria
changed the sheets; they had traces of
last night's man on them. Leon at the
desk had told Maria '301' never took
the same man up twice, because of
this the lobby boy referred to her as
'the black widow.' After Maria made
the bed 'Moonlight Sonata' started
playing again. Stuck on repeat; just
like everything else. Maria didn't
mind though, the drama was actually
growing on her. She took two plastic
cups from the bedside table, with some
red wine left in them. The rim of one of
them was covered in red lipstick. She
gently brushed a finger over it,
smudging the lipstick even more.
Strange how people never really
disappear, she thought, they always
leave some kind of trace behind. The
man had left traces on the sheets, the
woman had left traces on the cup.
Maria walked to the little bathroom,
to dispose of the wine before dropping

the cups in the bin liner. The minute
she opened the door she noticed
something was off. The lights were still
on and there was a strange smell
coming from the room. When she
looked to the right her stomach turned.
The woman of room 301 was floating
in the tub, her hair long and wavy, her
lips as red as the water that
surrounded her. She looked like an
angel with closed eyes. Maria did not
scream, she just dropped the cups.

Frida's Garden

Levi liked the way the garden looked when it was raining. The way Frida's tree, the one she had planted when they had moved into the house all those years ago, soaked up the puddles that were forming at its foot. It had been raining for days now and he had been sitting in the kitchen for hours at an end, watching the world disappear through the kitchen window.

The garden just wasn't the same without her. The roses had died last winter and the grass had turned brown the summer before. Levi raised himself from his chair and put the kettle on while the wind pulled at the kitchen doors. At least with her around it seemed like he knew what he was doing. Now that she was gone, he was once again a man without a plan.

It was autumn and he always missed her most when the leaves started falling again. People weren't supposed to be on their own when the world was as dark a place as it was in autumn. The world was getting smaller with every raindrop that hit the stained windows until it completely disappeared.

Highway 59

I am watching people pass by on the
interstate. Thousands of destinations,
the sun lighting up their faces.
A woman in a Dodge is texting while
she passes us by. A grandma with a
perm sips from a can of Mountain dew
in a Honda Civic that used to be white.
When I was a kid I didn't really believe
in the existence of a world outside of
my own. Life was like a
computer game. The streets, the
people, the buildings, they would all
pop up when I entered the space they
inhabited, like slowly generating pixels
just outside my view; a millions
destinations, a million beating hearts.

The Bedroom Window

Ironically enough she was hanging out
of the window the first time we met
and I remember thinking she might
fall out of it if she wasn't careful.
She did not seem to mind, or perhaps
she never saw the danger. Some people
are like that; remain like that for the
rest of their lives. They burn the candle
at both ends while the rest of us just
grow old. She was smoking a cigarette
and her hair was tied together in a
messy bun the day I was introduced to
her. Everything about her was messy.
The way her apartment looked, with
books scattered across the floor and
radiator, the way she was dressed,
layers of floral prints and knitwear,
no bra. She did not believe in bras, or
so she said. When I got to know her
I learned that she didn't believe in a
lot of things; in God, in discipline, in
the government. She didn't believe in
life either, and so one day they found
her on the street after she had jumped
from a window, her brains splattered
on the ice cold pavement, the snow
melting around her floral printed mess.

Ophelia

The rotten leaves cast a nasty smell on
the black water. She dreamed about
having legs but when she dreamed a bit
more realistically she dreamed about
him carrying her to the water so she
could die in his arms. He wouldn't hear
of it though, so she finally stopped
asking one day. He found her behind
the house one morning, floating in
nothing more than a floral blouse, like
a modern-day Ophelia, her spirit as
broken as her spinal cord.

For Yasinne

I had moved out to the city only a
month before and didn't know anyone
there, except for the people I shared the
house with. It was still very early when
I made my way through the stream of
commuters that needed to get to work.
My eyes were on the pavement as usual
when I heard my name. It took me a
second to recognize it. I had been
answering to it my entire life but
somehow it sounded very
foreign to me at that moment. It was
like it did not belong to me and the
word was directed at someone else; at
another girl on the street, a stranger
with a life more exciting than my own.
But it was my name and someone was
waiting for me to answer to it. So I
looked up and recognized my
room-mate. I don't know why, but I
reached out for him and our hands met.
For a second there I felt truly
connected. As if the entire week had
come down to this point, a Friday
morning in October, on a rainy street
in a city filled with strangers; and
everything made sense again.

Thirty Something

I look at myself in the mirror, traces of
wear and tear, decay. Shallow lines next
to my eyes, very subtle, but still there,
my breasts less firm than they used to
be, my stomach, my arms, my tired
face. I stare at my naked body, the body
that used to have a boyish youthfulness
over it. I stare at my body and it scares
the shit out of me.

Abigail

I had not seen her in years. She had a
child now, it had not been planned; she
wasn't done living her own life yet. Her
child was a girl, three years of age. I
remember her playing in my sink when
she was still a chubby baby. She was a
little lady now, with long brown hair
and blue eyes. When we walked to the
bus stop she kept stuffing things in my
hand, little treasures; a small purple
flower, a feather, an acorn.
Her mother's phone rang when we
reached the destination. I picked the
little girl up and started swinging her
in the air, like an airplane or a bird or a
piece of paper blown across the street
by the wind. She started shrieking and
smiling and after I got a bit
light-headed I put her down and she
started tickling me with the feather.
She clung to me when the bus
approached. I turned towards her
mother, trying to give her a final piece
of advice before I left but immediately
feeling like a dick for doing so.
I realized I still tried to fix her, because
if I could fix her, maybe I could fix
myself as well.

Dying Twice

I felt strange all of a sudden, like I knew I was about to die. I couldn't put my finger on it exactly but it was there and it hammered against my skull until my hands started sweating and it felt like I was fainting. They say once you accepted your death you stop being panicky, but I hadn't accepted my death yet, I probably never would. It was there though, hovering over all our heads like a siren song; beautiful, inevitable. The wind was pushing against the vehicle, while the rain spat at us with a mocking voice. I closed my eyes and imagined the little beads of sweat on the driver's forehead. This calmed me down a little. At least we would die together. I can't think of anything more depressing than dying alone. I started to regret my life, the choices I hadn't made, chances I didn't take. What I regretted most though was the feeling that you would never know how much I cared for you, how much I loved you, how much I wanted to be there where you were, all

the time, even those times when I told
you to leave, the times you actually left,
the times you were so angry at me that
you spat fire. I braced myself for the
impact when the bus started slipping,
the tires screeching loudly just before
we disappeared over the guardrail.
Remember me, I thought, remember
me so that I don't have to die twice.

Lost in the Supermarket

"Why me?" she asked, tying back her hair. "I don't know," he shrugged, but she could tell that he did. He glanced at her and she smiled at him in the mirror. "I guess you looked scared, you know?" She turned away from the dressing table to face him. "Like a child lost in a supermarket." He left a long pause, which he often did in between sentences; if he ever talked at all. "Except the world was your supermarket."

You smell funny

That particular morning smelled of vomit and decay. The flannel had been drenched in cheap soap because none of the patients would notice anyway. Mrs C looked at her with eyes like saucers. "I lie in my own shit and I can't help myself." Her face looked hollow, her skin had lost all of its softness, but her eyes were like the ocean; two bright blue irises around the rotten pupils. "You don't smell like yourself," he said when she pressed her backside against his dick that night. He smelled her neck, ignoring her soft lower half against his loins. "You smell old, like the people you take care of." Her hair looked dull and the spark that used to live in her eyes, the one he loved so very much, had disappeared completely.

The Boy with the Scar
on his Heart

Do you remember that time when we
walked to the supermarket and they
were playing latin music on the street
and you started dancing like nobody
was watching, grabbing me by the
hands and pulling me close. I'm sorry I
was such a self aware piece of shit that
day. I wish I had danced with you, I
wish I'd done a lot of things with you.

The Pond

She had been sitting at the window the
entire morning, trying to read a book
but failing to do so because she could
not make her mind focus on the words
that were dancing in front of her eyes.
It was autumn and she had been ill
for a long time now. I looked up from
my own book, unable to concentrate.
I had been watching her. I had never
seen her skin so pale, it was like she
was transparent, like she was already
disappearing. The pond in our front
garden was one of the reasons we had
bought the house. She loved it there.
I had been wheeling her out there all
the time so that she could read, with
a blanket over her legs and a flask of
coffee. She no longer went out into the
garden; the wind tore her apart
nowadays.

The Day my Grandfather lost his Words

I remember a story my father once told
me about my grandfather. I never met
the man for he died long before my
mother gave birth to me.
My grandfather was a silent man,
driving my grandmother to despair
with his absence of words. I think this
is why she cheated on him in the end.
Or perhaps it is just what the women in
our family do, their hearts are pressed
against their rib cage for so long that
their love eventually pours out in every
possible direction.

For a Good Man

I reluctantly put my key in our
apartment door. As long as I stay on
this side of the entrance, nothing will
have changed, your belongings will still
be there, you'll be sitting behind the
computer playing some video game
and we will have a coffee together to
discuss both our days. I sigh, one can
only bury ones head in the sand for so
long and I had already been putting
this off for a week, fleeing to another
country with nothing but a couple of
t-shirts and a toothbrush in my pack.
No grand plans, no schedules, no
nothing. I turn the key and listen to the
familiar click which grants me access.
The lights are off and it's cold upstairs.
I wait a little longer before I slowly
climb the stairs. This is the first time in
six years you're not waiting for me to
come home.

Parting Gift

The boy I once loved was no longer
there. I could see it in his eyes, how
they no longer stared back at mine,
light blue like the ocean in the travel
magazines I used to buy when I still
thought I was going places. I could see
it in the way he crossed the street, the
way his feet hit the concrete, confident,
self-assured. There was no room for me
in his heart anymore. I tried, I really
did, I just wanted you to know.

Choking on the Dust

As I watch the remnants of a life that no longer belongs to me burn, I feel a lump settle in the back of my throat. Your face will start to fade, just like it does when someone's been dead for a while. You don't want it to happen but it does anyway and there's no point in holding on. I watch the fabric of the floral dress I wore in Paris slowly turn to dust. The letter you wrote me on the day we first met burns so fast that it feels like it never even existed in the first place. Fire does not discriminate. I watch the melting snow around the pit getting contaminated by black ashes before it completely disappears. Six years of my life diminished to a pile of dust in a matter of seconds. I imagine the pile of dust I'll leave behind one day. An entire life for the flowers to grow on. Eternity, eternity, eternity.

The Englishman and the Lady from across the Sea

They only met in public places, the Englishman and the lady from across the sea. It was safer that way, she had told him. They were sitting opposite of each other in a small café overlooking the Thames. She was still laughing at a remark he had made while he lit his fifth cigarette. The sun had transformed the colour of her skin; it was golden, except for the narrow band of skin around her ring finger.

Bus Stop

"It's okay," she said, when the boy
noticed his mistake. He had been
telling a story to some girl he was
trying to impress and he had hit the
girl outside the shelter with a hand
gesture he had used to put some drama
into his story. She was wearing a green
woolen coat and was standing right
outside of the shelter at the bus stop
down our street. The upper part of
her scarf was covered in little drops of
condensed breath. The bus had been
delayed. When she walked up to the
bus stop it had been snowing and after
she glanced at the people who were
taking shelter there she decided to stay
outside. She couldn't bear their
conversations, the way they laughed
into their phones, the way young girls
tried getting the attention of young
boys. So she stood outside, with snow
in her hair and on her shoulders; a
swan queen surrounded by morons.

The Halls were Empty

The people were gone now.
The halls were empty.
She found herself alone,
trying to cling on to the pictures
of their faces
whilst listening to the ticking
of the clock
they had left behind.
Funny how time changed it all.
She had never really liked them,
but now that they were gone,
she couldn't do much else
but miss them.

Golden

I've been here before. Like this, drunk,
watching the floral curtains that cover
up their perfect mess. I wonder what it
would be like to sleep with him. I like
slipping into other people's lives as if
they were my own, feeling the fabric of
their clothes on my skin, tasting their
wine, fucking their husbands.
I turn around and look at myself in
their mirror. The black pools
underneath my eyes had gotten much
worse since the last time I'd checked.
When I walk out I can see them sitting
there, at the dinner table, miserable as
fuck in the little golden cage they built
for themselves. I walk up their stairs
and look at the mess I made. I will have
to clean up before they get home.

Mostly Sober

She likes lighting their cigarette;
the poets, the artists, the lost boys
staggering around the pub in their
quest to self destruct. They beg for
cigarettes, for attention, for a piece
of arse. She likes turning her back at
them, like they had done with her
when she was younger. There's a man
with dark hair pointing at her in a
very dramatic gesture, his hands on
his heart as she gets up to leave. She
buttons her coat and lights her own
cigarette. It's time to go home.

The roof that needed fixing

He had built the house himself before
his father died. When they started
working on it the old man fell from the
roof, grabbed his left arm, opened his
mouth and died. The younger man did
not finish the roof until two months
later. As he sat in his father's chair, one
year older than his father was when
he died, he looked at the rain pouring
down the woodwork and onto the
carpet. He was a father now, but his
children had left him as they no longer
felt the need to listen to his stories,
his promises, the dreams he never
chased. "You should fix that leak," his
wife repeated every other week, until
she eventually left him too. In the end
it just collapsed on him. When they
found him, he was still sitting in his
father's reading chair, his mouth wide
open and rays of sunlight touching his
cracked open head.

Saturday Night

And just like that
we became strangers again,
living under the same roof,
like we had done before,
silent glances,
locked up words,
and I hated you for it.

Scheveningen

I remember you telling me
your father died
when you were just a child,
causing your brother
to lose all the colour from his hair
for a year.
The waves made our footsteps shrink.
I remember cold feet. Sinking feet.
Stars. Dogs with little lights
stuck on their collars
sniffing at each other's butts.
They're much more honest than people
when you think about it.
Girls dimming their lights
when reaching the shoreline.
The letter I wrote
to my dead grandfather.
Hot chocolate. Pianos. A kid shouting.
S without her clothes on, being the first
to disappear in the waves. Air planes.
Lots of couples clinging on to each
other for dear life. People meeting on
the boulevard. Pitch black skies
colliding with crashing waves.

Between the Pines

It was not until
I dared to look up,
past the black sky
and behind the canopy
that I realized
the drumming sound
had been coming
from my own chest
the whole time.

Unheimlich

She emptied the contents of her
stomach into the sink that morning.
The girl looked at herself in the mirror
as she wiped her mouth.
The Germans had a word for the state
she was in. *Unheimlich.*
It was in the familiarity of the people
who surrounded her, the comfort of a
job she could rely on, it was in the
patterns of the brown tiles near the
sink. A second wave of nausea hit her
as her pager went off. Someone had
forgotten to bring Mrs L her stockings.

Going to Pieces
on your Kitchen Floor

I notice I am stalling,
even though
you already went away
hours ago,
when I was still half asleep
on the other side of your bed,
waking up
with your hand on my cheek
as you kissed me goodbye
for the last time.

12.47

A half finished ham sandwich
in an Air France wrapper,
spread with too much butter.
An empty plastic cup
with brown stains
on the rim
where my lips touched it.
A middle-aged couple
with two empty bottles of wine
on their fold-up tables.
The woman sitting next to me
nervously scratches off
her blue nail polish
while the airplane
starts on its descent.
The sun only shines
above the clouds today.

Fuck You and
Fuck the White Horse
You Rode in on

Today I decided to pretend
you are dead,

so that I no longer
have someone
to project
these childish
romantic fantasies
upon

and I can continue to live life
like a grown-up
all battered and bruised,
with a heart
made of stone

and I never felt this alone.

The Zombie Apocalypse

They were just sitting there,
scattered across the small room,
waiting to die.

They sat in front
of the television
during the day
and shat their pants
during the night.

And still, when the music played
they got up from their chairs
recreating the steps
they used to take
in their lover's arms.

The Orchid

The middle one
was an orchid
and it was broken in two
when grandad buried it
for the second time
with its roots dangling
in the wind,
little bits of sand
landing everywhere
when the window was open
and the curtain came flying in.

Rebecca Rijsdijk

Please be quiet

"Just do what you feel like doing,"
she said

as if it were a choice
instead of a luxury
(only a few of us could afford).

Everything about her
pissed me off that morning,
perhaps because it was easier
that way.

I looked at her,
moving her hand in the wind
enjoying the force
with which it pushed
against her skin.

I found myself
envying her youth
and wondered
how I had grown
into something so old,
something so responsible,
something with such a bitter lining
and such a heavy heart.

Gods

The names
on the windows,
in the magazines,
on billboards,
of people who made it,
people who are celebrated,
worshipped,
honoured,
make me choke
on my own frustration,
spit, vomit, rage,
foam,
like a mad dog.

Put me down.
Put me down.

Day Trips

I can't wait for it to rain
so that the woods
will clear out
and the scum
of the earth,
on their Sunday biking trips,
their children in strollers,
their dogs on leashes,
will go home
and sit on their couch
in front of the fucking television
where they belong
and I can ride my bike
to and from work
in peace again.

Where Flowers
had carved their Way
through the Tarmac

I noticed I was daydreaming
by the time I reached the spot
where flowers had carved
their way through the tarmac.

A couple of staples
kept my bag from falling apart
and I had buttoned my coat all wrong.

Jazz records

I listen to the noises
the house makes.

My neighbours are waking up,
the men they are with
are waking up.

I smell their coffee,
their first cigarettes,
hear their laughter.

They take showers together,
have breakfast together,
listen to jazz records together

while I just lay here,
in the dark,

listening to the wind
tearing up the roof.

I told you I was a Twat but You wouldn't listen

He sits on the bed,
naked as a new born baby,
a cigarette in his hand,
smoke floating away
toward the bedroom window,
listening to some heavy metal
while his tears fall on my pillow.

Suburbia

And she just sat there
in her little doll's house,
expecting a giant hand
to come in through the window
any time now,
rearranging the furniture
and smashing in
her husband's head
as she peeled off
all the skin
around her fingernails.

Milk and Honey

She rode toward the sunset
in her father's worn down car.
A breeze picked up strands
of her hair
through the open window;
while a cigarette burned
between her lips.

He told her stories
of milk and honey

as he replaced the grass
with mud.

Life is what happens to You when You are too busy sticking your Head up your Arse

Sometimes my feet are so heavy
that it feels like
I should leave them behind
in order to get to work in time.

I keep telling myself
that I am living a life
which doesn't belong to me

to discover in the end,
that it is the only life I ever lived.

Floating

There are people
up in the air,
clinging on
to their little woven baskets,
staring at the warmth
that keeps them floating.

They're looking down
on the rest of us

while we stumble
over each other

like a bunch of fucking ants.

For a Good Man (2)

Last night,
when our neighbour thought
our television had fallen over,
and it was actually a plate
crashing to the floor
giving birth
to a million little pieces,
(we need new china),
when I trashed my wedding dress,
with such force
that the lid of the bin
broke off,
(white fabric spilling over the edges)
when I screamed at you
that I wanted to die
because I hated everything,
(and you cried
because I was such a fucking bitch)
I really just loved you.

12.00

An ambulance,
the wind,
church bells,
voices on the pavement,
a train leaving the station,
an air plane,
a broken faucet,
a dog,
your hands
always on the keyboard.

I love you
even when you don't notice me.

A Razor
and some Cologne

She was looking
for her dead father's belongings

small things
that told something
about the person
who had owned them,
little hints that he had been there.

A razor, some cologne.

But there was nothing left
in the house
which reminded her of him;
like he had never even been there
in the first place.

Distant Shores

The only people out here
at this time of night
are the mad ones.

The ones
who walk into the sea
naked,

to disappear
in the black waves
and end up
on distant shores.

Home town

The way you drag
your miserable arses
to church every Sunday.

The way you wash
your estate cars
every Saturday
before having coffee
with the in-laws.

The way you make
a couple of children
because God told you to do so.

The way you stay
with wives you hate,
with husbands you despise.

The way you die
in the exact same house
you were born in.

It just breaks
my fucking heart.

Dutch

So I did my best
to be nice
when you caught up with me
on your bike,
and all you did was smile
because you had just seen me
remove my bra
through my sleeve again.

The Cardigan

She remembered,
back when she was in love with him
and she really wasn't supposed to,
she remembered the hug he gave her
at the top of the stairs.

He was wearing an old knitted rag,
the sleeves were far too long,
covering half of his hands
as he held her close,
for just a second or two
because they were both
decent human beings.

Athens

Stray dogs, street musicians.
There's a girl
sitting on the pavement
eating her lunch
while screwing up her eyes
to keep the sun out.
I follow the French up the mountain,
the higher we go,
the smaller the buildings get
until they are nothing
but little white pebbles
thrown against the misty hills.

Ruined Shower Curtains

I remember your eager head
when you disappeared
underneath the sheets,
the convict neighbour
who stole flowers for me
from the gardens of the elderly,
the two trees in front of our house,
the yellow walls,
the church bells,
on a Sunday morning.

I remember your face
when it was happy,
the smell of rain on the pavement,
the conversations at the kitchen table,
the books piled up against the doors
that never opened anymore.

I remember ruined shower curtains
after I slipped on my razor blade.

But most of all
I remember your heart
on the floor
right after I stomped on it

and I am sorry.

Cat Town

There's a little park
 in the northern part of the city
ruled by stray cats.

I watch them stretch themselves
against the trees.

They live in little skyscrapers
built by homeless men
who drink beer all day.

Porch Light

I go out in the garden every night now,
shaking like a son of a bitch
because it is too cold
to go out after the sun goes down.
But the stars are so nice
and my last cigarette is so nice
and the sounds the trees make when
they rid themselves
of last season's leaves are so nice.
My mother comes out
and switches on the porch light.
Everything disappears.
Nice.

Happy

It all came falling down
as soon as she opened the door
to his apartment.
The bloodshed eyes,
the suicidal thoughts,
the old skin peeled of
like that of a snake
as she sat there alone,
in the dark,
thinking about
what she wanted to be
in spite of all the things
that had happened to her
in what seemed like ten lifetimes,
and in that moment,
she was happy.

ABOUT THE AUTHOR

Rebecca grew up in the woods behind her parents' house in Holland but now made London her home. She studied photography at the Royal Academy of Art in The Hague, where she soon realized that she was more interested in words than images. 'Portraits of Girls' is the author's first substantial collection of works.

'Reading these portraits is like staring at a wounding moment suspended forever in a photograph. The painful aches of growing up and growing old, of finding your identity and then losing it again; of searching for your place in the world, only to find that you don't really feel at home anywhere, or only feel at home while on the move, or miss a home that doesn't exist, cannot exist anymore, and maybe never really existed; of searching for kindred spirits in other people and discovering that love and hate are difficult, but it's abandonment and banality and lost opportunities that tend to kill you slowly. It's all there, and it's painful and beautiful.'

Sofia Romualdo

'Each story is a tiny little truth that adds up to so much more. In this collection are vignettes that you want to be part of: tender, awkward, uncomfortable, bittersweet, always a little painful. You'll want to linger in each one, staying in Rebecca's head just a little longer, even though you can't wait to see what's around the next corner. After a while, you'll wonder if these aren't really just bits and pieces of your own memory.'

George Song

'This book is so compelling I felt like I had gained a new lifelong friend after finishing every single one of the short stories. In just a few words Rebecca manages to capture entire lives. Lives full of misery and joy, full of experiences and memories I'll never know anything about but which feel as if they're now inherently a part of my life. In just a few sentences she somehow manages to take you on emotional rollercoasters, picking you up and dragging you along spectacularly to drop you off again just as suddenly. Leaving you astonished, amazed, saddened or moved in any other way. Often stories start seemingly innocent, with little, everyday moments which soon turn into something way more meaningful. This is one of those books I'll end up picking up again and again, imagining myself in the worlds surrounding these moments or to see if maybe there is more to be found in these words I've already read so often. To see if maybe there is something I had missed before.'

Isabella Prins

'A great read, except for the bits where she swears a lot.'

Mum

Made in the USA
Charleston, SC
27 April 2016